THE BUTTERFLY BENEATH THE EARTH

A Dark Gothic Medieval Paranormal Romance Novella

Lisa Shea

Copyright © 2020 by Lisa Shea / Minerva Webworks LLC
All rights reserved.
Cover design by Lisa Shea
Book design by Lisa Shea

No part of this book may be reproduced in any form or by any electronic or mechanical means including information storage and retrieval systems, without permission in writing from the author. The only exception is by a reviewer, who may quote short excerpts in a review.

The bulk of this book is a work of fiction. Names, characters, places, and incidents either are products of the author's imagination or are used fictitiously. The sections based on real individuals and locations are researched to the best of the author's ability.

~ v1 ~

Visit my website at LisaShea.com

The Butterfly Beneath The Earth was originally published in episodic format as part of the Amazon Vella platform.

Honey is dear bought if licked off thorns.

12th Century Proverb

THE BUTTERFLY
BENEATH
THE EARTH

Contents

Chapter One 1
Chapter Two 13
Chapter Three 17
Chapter Four 25
Chapter Five 33
Chapter Six 39
Chapter Seven 47
Chapter Eight 51
Chapter Nine 61
Chapter Ten 67
Dedication 76
About the Author 77
Free Books 78

Chapter One

Lincoln, England 1218

*"It is during our darkest moments
that we must focus to see the light."
~ Aristotle*

The larger bee embraced its dead companion in a tight grip, efficiently lifting it up out of the densely-packed hive. It flew a short distance away from the bustling community and unceremoniously dropped the body on a mound of dirt. Its task done, it looped in a circle to head back into the hive, scanning each worker for any sign of weakness or injury.

I brushed a loose strand of my long, auburn hair back into its braid. I'd been tending to these bees for ten long years now – ever since my parents had sold me to become Elric's wife. Elric the Beekeeper had been twenty years my senior, and while I hadn't loved him, I was grateful that he had never abused me.

For those first five years, Elric had trained me day and night on the intricacies of bees. He had explained in excruciating detail how their hierarchies worked. One class of bees would gather nectar. Another class would tend to the young. The Queen, of course, ruled all with an iron grip.

And then there were the cleaners. The ones who watched for any indication that one of their hive-members was not able to pull their weight. The moment the ailing bee came to a rest, the cleaner would toss them out of the hive. Finished, done, not another thought.

As I had been by my parents, the moment I turned fourteen.

I blew out my breath. I turned away from the hive.

The bright July sun beat down on the meadow, reflecting heat up in dense waves. The lush fragrance of honeysuckle and dog rose was nearly sickening. I could barely breathe.

I knew I was not like other people. I'd grown up in my family's small butcher shop. Maybe my nose had become maladjusted over time; it clearly interacted with the world in a way most found to be strange. Floral scents were smothering and sickly sweet. In comparison, I found comfort in the earthy scents. Scents of ripe meat. Dense dirt.

The aroma of blood simmering over a fire. To me, those were the scents which were comforting.

The scents meant home. My *real* home.

I sighed as I looked across the meadow of wildflowers. This landscape felt completely alien, so different from the tightly-packed city streets I had grown up in. Even after ten years, this world felt unreal. Untethered. A hallucinatory state from which I might someday finally wake.

I didn't belong here.

My husband, while not physically abusive, had always been disappointed in my inability to instantly fit in to his world. He had expected me to effortlessly take the place of his first wife, Griselda, who had died in childbirth. After our first few months together, when his courtship behavior faded, Elric reverted to his true nature. He found an opportunity every day to point out my *brokenness*. To make an effort to *fix* me.

And now …

I walked across the meadow to the small stable alongside the cottage and pulled the heavy door open. Rohesia was still in her stall, her baleful gaze clearly showing her displeasure at missing out on the beautiful morning sunshine. I saddled and bridled her. Then I carefully filled her saddle-bags with the latest batch of fresh beeswax candles, making sure each lay ensconced in a fold of fabric. Not a dent could mar them.

I led Rohesia out, closed up the stables, and mounted up. At the edge of the clearing, I stopped as I always did by the split-trunk apple tree. It had been Juliana's favorite place in the world for her four short years of life. Now she lay there in eternal rest, nestled in its roots.

Her father's body was right there alongside her.

I headed off down the trail. A few rises of land, and Lincoln Castle became a glimmer on the horizon, its city spread out around it. I had to draw much closer before I could make out the activity of construction and repairs. Our valiant sheriff Nicholaa de la Haye had remained strong during the siege, doing whatever it took to protect our castle from the French, even though she was well into her sixties. Unfortunately, the city dwellers below fared less well. The chaos and looting in the aftermath was being called "Lincoln's Fair", although it was no fair celebration to those whose homes had been burned, their possessions pillaged.

It was one of the times I was grateful that my own cottage was safely tucked out against the woods. Unseen. Unnoticed.

The farmland turned to bustling streets, and after various twists and turns I pulled in alongside the butcher shop. My mother would never let me hear the end of it if I did not at least stop in to pay my respects. I gave Rohesia's reins a quick loop around the post and stepped in.

The familiar, thick smells washed over me.

I laid a fond hand against the doorframe as I looked around the room. The two-story structure was made of thick, firm oak. The tables, the benches, all could stand up to heavy usage and the hot scouring necessary to keep stains from setting. My great-grandfather had built this place, and each male child in turn had wielded the axe and knife.

The female children … well, they were unnecessary. They took up space. They were to be sold off as soon as possible, so the son could better maintain the family heritage.

And so my younger brother was the filet, while I was the hoof.

My mother looked up from where she had her arms immersed, full to the elbow, in a massive pot of blood. She was checking for solids, I knew, as it slowly warmed over the fire. She nodded her head. "On your way to the Cathedral, Constance?" Her face was lined and her hair was already full gray. She was solidly plump, a luxury not enjoyed by most in the city around us.

My father's rough cough sounded from the back room. I could almost see his stout body shake with the noise. "A' course she is. Those beeswax candles are too good for the likes of us."

I sighed. "I've told you before, if you would wish some candles for -"

My mother snorted. "As if we need such high-born airs. We have more than enough tallow candles and can afford to burn them morning to night! Besides, who can even smell their sharpness amidst all of this?" She took her crimson hands from the pot and waved them in the air, spreading droplets all over the dirt floor.

I nodded. The sleeping chambers were up on the second floor, and the mere flight of stairs did little to remove the inhabitants from the stench of the place. Or so, at least, Anabel had told me every time she visited.

Me, I couldn't smell a thing out of place. It was simply home.

My mother dove her hands back into the cauldron. "By the way, did you hear Lucan is temporary Reeve, with Bartholomew's broken leg? Can you imagine?"

Just the name Lucan was enough to send a tremor of mixed emotion through me, but my mother meant Lucan the enforcer from Waddington, not *the* Lucan, not the boy from my childhood.

Not the one who had vowed -

I stepped back. "The priests aren't known for their patience. I'll see you both at the Summer Faire."

My mother nodded her head, her attention already back on the blood and bile.

My stomach twisted as I climbed back onto Rohesia.

Lucan.

There had been a time that the mere mention of that name would send me into fluttering butterflies and swooning delight. But then I had turned fourteen and my parents had led me to the cathedral. They had placed my hand into that of a man twenty years my senior.

There was no going back.

I wended my way through the streets, past half-rebuilt houses and remnants of tumbled-down wells, until I reached the outskirts of Lincoln Cathedral. I knew the towering structure had taken a full hundred-and-fifty years to build. My grandfather had boasted to any within earshot that he had been an honored guest at its opening ceremony. Our butcher shop had supplied the priests and bishops countless chops of lamb, beef, and pork.

And meanwhile the city-folk often struggled by on gruel and meal.

The enormous stone edifice had always seemed forbidding to me – towering, dark, all sharp angles and pointed spires. Returning Crusaders told that it was the tallest building they had ever seen, no matter which country they crossed.

I believed it.

I skirted the edge of the massive cathedral, crossing myself out of habit, and at last reached the large stables. A boy, a rough lad of twelve, nodded in familiar greeting to me, taking Rohesia's reins as I dismounted. I carefully retrieved my wares and then headed along the cobblestone pathway to the cathedral's back entrance. It stood open against the summer heat, and I quickly moved through it.

While my beeswax candles stood up to the heat far better than fat-based tallow ones, they still could wilt and bend. I knew the priests demanded perfection. I would not give them any excuse to haggle the price.

Father Godwinson was waiting for me in his elegant office. His tunic featured embroidered gold circles against the finest white linen. A fringe of gray hair circled his head like a halo, but I knew not to be fooled by that. The man was as miserly as an alewife at the end of a long, hard winter.

He glanced up from his parchments.

The Butterfly Beneath the Earth

The cathedral's bells sounded out noon.

He nodded in satisfaction. "Punctual, as always, Constance."

I stepped forward and carefully laid my saddle bags on the wolfskin rug. I drew out the slender, pale-yellow tapers and placed them in a neat row on his polished wood desk.

His slender fingers were nearly as sallow as the candles as he went one by one down the row, carefully rolling each one to inspect it from all angles. One would have thought he was preparing to eat them, rather than simply burn them to ash.

At last he nodded. "Exemplary. Your husband trained you well."

I pressed my lips together, saying nothing.
Here it came.

His brow furrowed in a show of compassion which didn't reach his eyes. "Speaking of which, Constance, you know that our offer still stands, to move your daughter to our graveyard. Surely she should lie for her eternal rest in hallowed ground."

His smile grew. "As I have mentioned, we would not even require any monetary offering for this precious blessing. A simple monthly donation of one hundred of your finest -"

I kept my voice cool. Father Godwinson was my most important customer and I could not afford to shake the hive. "Your beneficence is beyond measure, Father Godwinson. I am truly touched by your generosity." I let my gaze fall. "However, as you know, my husband, God rest his soul, was absolutely determined to keep his daughter's grave within sight of our cottage."

Father Godwinson waved a hand in the air. "Yes, yes. And now with his untimely end, so hard on the heels of your daughter's accident -"

My arms crossed of their own accord. My tone became rough. "Are the candles to your satisfaction?"

His brows came down, forming a sharp V, but he nodded. "Quite."

He reached beneath his desk and took out a small iron box. From a leather pouch on his belt he withdrew a key, and in a moment the box was open. He removed the small piece of parchment lying on top. Then he took the quill from his desk stand, dipped it in the inkwell, and made a notation on the parchment. At last he carefully counted out the coins for me, one by one.

I patiently waited until he fully withdrew his hand. Father Godwinson was a man who treasured routine and ceremony. It would not do to interrupt one moment of this ritual.

When he had settled both hands back into his lap, I nodded. I reached forward to gather up the coins into my hands. I carefully slid them into the leather bag on my hip. I gave him a short curtsey. "Until a fortnight, Father Godwinson."

I began to turn -

He raised that claw-like hand again. His fingernails could have been made from wax, they were so translucent. "Oh, there is one more thing."

I stilled. For Father Godwinson to break his routine was for a blazing comet to cross a clear summer's sky.

Father Godwinson's voice rose high, becoming a clarion call. "Oh, reeve? Could you come here, please?"

My blood iced.

Bartholomew was the cruelest man I had ever met. The only reason he continued to be re-elected reeve was that any in Lincoln who spoke out against him found their barns mysteriously burned down or their horses suddenly gone lame. In most cities a reeve was a protector, tasked with watching over the safety of the inhabitants within.

Here in Lincoln, our reeve was a nightmare incarnate.

Reeve Bartholomew's visit to my cottage after my husband's passing was brutally etched in my mind. At the time, I was ravaged by grief. Not so much for the loss of my husband – he was often cold and demanding – but at the totality of everything crashing down on my head. My daughter's tragedy. The uproar caused by my husband's refusal to bury her in sanctified ground. His obsession with her freshly-turned grave, overarching all else.

And now he had cut his own throat, pouring his life's blood down to her in what appeared, to all observers, to be some sort of a dark pagan ritual.

The reeve had taken one look at my husband's dead body, one look at me, and made the situation clear. Either I gave myself to him fully, or the official report of *suicide* would be changed to that of suspicious death. Maybe even that of heretical ceremony.

My daughter's young body would be dug up from the earth, hung in an iron gibbet, and displayed as an example of the wickedness of sin.

I would not let that happen.

I *could* not let that happen.

And so I had stepped forward to the reeve -

From behind me, a throat cleared.

I clenched my fists and turned to stare at the open doorway. I steeled myself for the ox-muscled build – the sharp, black eyes –

A man stepped into the entryway.

I staggered back against the desk.

Lucan.

Chapter Two

Lucan.

His shoulders were broader than I remembered. He had to be, what, twenty-eight? Four years older than me. In the decade since I'd seen him last, he'd hardened. It was both the lean muscles of his arms and something in his eyes. His dark hair was loose to his shoulders, and his leather armor clearly had seen heavy use. A sword now hung at his hip.

A distant corner of my mind reminded me that my mother had mentioned Lucan was temporarily filling in as reeve for Bartholomew. But I'd never imagined it was *this* Lucan.

My Lucan.

I managed to say, "I thought you were still in the Holy Land."

His face could have been carved from granite. "I've arrived in Lincoln only this morning. How is your husband?"

Father Godwinson's tone took on a caustic edge. "Elric, sorry to say, lost his faith in God our Savior. The heretic committed suicide. He now is eternally damned in Hell's raging fires."

Fury and sorrow dove at each other's throats, and my breath left me –

Lucan was there at my elbow, holding me up.

Father Godwinson tapped his fingers on his carved desk. "In any case, Lucan, this is the woman I was telling you about. The chandler. Our official candlemaker. You will take her with you on your queries. It is of the utmost importance that this be handled quickly. The outrage must be brought to an end."

I still could not rein in my tumbling thoughts. I barely whispered the word. "Outrage?"

Father Godwinson drew himself up to his full height. His gaze became steely. "Someone has stolen my engraved silver candle-holder from the sacristy."

* * *

I was walking down the stone hallways, out into the bright summer sunshine, and I only blinked into awareness as we reached the stables. Lucan's voice lifted in a low laugh. "Could it be? Rohesia's still alive? God's teeth, she must be -"

"Nearly twenty," I agreed, seeming to breathe for the first time. "She was my parents' wedding gift to me."

His gaze shuttered, and he looked away.

When he spoke, his voice was tighter. "I've been tasked with tracking down the thief. Top priority. Father Godwinson feels this blasphemy is an affront to God himself."

I nodded. I had no doubt that Father Godwinson had used those very words.

Lucan turned to look out through the open gates. "Father Godwinson gave me a list of potential suspects to question. First, Olvin the Beggar –"

I sighed. "Father Godwinson is referring to Olvin the Cobbler."

Lucan blinked in surprise. "What? Olvin was one of the best cobblers in the city, when I left. What happened?"

I turned my attention to Rohesia. The stable-boy had finished saddling her and was holding her reins. I muttered, "Father Godwinson tripped and fell in the snow last Michaelmas. He blamed it on his boot's sole. Olvin was fined for every last penny he owned."

Lucan's lips pressed.

A stable boy brought over Lucan's steed.

I blinked in surprise.

The horse was magnificent. His black coat shone with gloss and health. The saddle and reins were finely worked. And it almost seemed as if the seat was embossed with forget-me-nots –

Lucan mounted in one smooth motion and turned his steed with easy familiarity. "Let's get started."

Chapter Three

Lucan and I were silent as we rode side by side out of the castle complex and through the dense city streets.

We were heading for the poorest section of town.

For most of his career Olvin the Cobbler had owned a well-respected shop on the main street, creating high-quality shoes in a variety of styles. His wares were always in demand.

And then had come the afternoon that Father Godwinson had slipped.

I took the lead as we reached the outskirts of the city, where the poorer shacks were clustered together. There, tucked in the very end, was Olvin's current residence.

We dismounted. Lucan took both sets of reins to walk them toward a birch tree, to tie them up.

I went up to the door of the one-room structure and knocked. I called out, "Olvin? It's Constance."

Olvin drew open the door with a warm smile. He was tall, slender, in his mid-forties. "Constance! It's great to see you! Always a pleasure. Thank you for the gift of the sheep skin. I was able to make several pairs of slippers from that."

I waved a hand. "My parents weren't going to use it anyway, and they didn't even ask what I wanted it for."

I reached into my pouch and drew out three short, squat candles. "These are to help when you need to do fine work."

He beamed. "My eyes get so bleary when I have to sew by tallow candles. With yours, I can work late into the night!"

I drew my head close. "Just so you know, I'm actually here on official business. The Reeve -"

Olvin drew back in concern, clutching the candles to his chest. "The Reeve? I don't want any trouble from him. Whatever Father Godwinson is saying -"

Lucan stepped up alongside me. "Hello there, Olvin."

Olvin blinked in surprise, and then he had Olvin in a full hug, laughing in pleasure. "Lucan! You're home! What has it been, ten years? What a pleasure!"

It was a long minute before Olvin stepped back to look him over. "You're filled out," he announced. "Got some meat on those bones, finally. The Crusades made a man out of you, that's for sure."

He blinked in surprise. "But Connie said the Reeve -"

Lucan nodded, a small smile on his lips. "I'd barely delivered my message to Lady Nicholaa when she made the request. Apparently Reeve Bartholomew had suffered an … an accident of some sort. With my experience in the Crusades, Lady Nicholaa asked if I could fill in until Bartholomew healed from his injuries."

Olvin's smile stretched from ear to ear. "I haven't heard better news in a year! Well then, come on in!"

We stepped in.

The space might have been a quarter the size of his former shop, but Olvin was a true professional. He had organized his available space with a careful eye. And it was clear that the townsfolk had rewarded him for his many years of service. I saw that most of his tools had already been replaced, and at least ten pairs of shoes were in various stages of construction.

Olvin saw my gaze and nodded. "I am so grateful for the support of the community. Even some of the other cobblers donated their spare tools to me, to help me restart. In another month, I should be able to afford a larger shop closer to the center."

Olvin turned to Lucan. "How have you been, lad? You must have seen some amazing places while you've been away!"

Lucan's gaze shadowed. He gave a quiet nod. "Let's leave that for another time, shall we? We are here to talk with you about a candlestick. A silver candlestick."

I stepped in. "It was part of the sacristy set, Olvin. Finely engraved with lilies."

Olvin stared at us as if we'd gone completely insane. At last he said, "You think Father Godwinson lets me get anywhere the sacristy?"

Lucan glanced at me.

I shook my head. "Father Godwinson maintains a strict order of precedence in his sermons. Only the most wealthy are allowed to sit up front. Then the merchants, then commoners. People like Olvin are barely allowed to squeeze in the back of the church."

Olvin snorted. "I couldn't have even told you they had lilies on them. I'm lucky I can see the gleam of light."

I asked him, "Has anybody unusual been asking for fancy shoes recently? Anything out of the ordinary? Maybe whoever stole the candlestick sold it for money."

Olvin chuckled. "They'd have had to sell it down in London. Father Godwinson has his spies everywhere. They'd see it if it showed up in any of our local shops."

I agreed with him on that point.

Olvin gave me a wink. "That younger brother of yours has come in three times in the past month, each for a different pair of women's boots, each in a different size. He's certainly … exploring his options."

My blush rose to my eyes.

Lucan turned to me in confusion. "Surely the kid's not old enough to wed yet. He was just a whelp when I left. How old is he now?"

"Drustan is eighteen." I rolled my shoulders. "He's heir to a thriving butcher shop. The number of girls throwing themselves at him ... competing for his affection …"

Lucan's eyes shuttered. I could almost hear his thoughts.

It's a different situation, if you're the eighteen-year-old son of a poor tenant farmer.

He said, more harshly than necessary, "I doubt that feckless boy is the thief. Does anyone else come to mind?"

Olvin shook his head. "Just the usual orders coming through." He gave a soft shrug. "Business has been fairly brisk, with everyone still recovering from the French siege. People have to replace items which were stolen or lost."

Lucan's gaze shadowed, "News of that assault travelled even to Europe. I am glad to see you both were unharmed."

Olvin nodded. "Lincoln was fortunate that more did not lose their lives. And, also, that Lady Nicholaa was so capable." He looked around. "We will rise up again, as we always do. We will help each other out and rebuild."

I saw a pair of green-dyed shoes to one side, just a bit smaller than my own. There were clovers embroidered on the ankles. Gentle humor lit me. "Are those for Anabel?"

He chuckled at that. "You know her well. Yes, they are. But she has no need for silver candlesticks. She has … other sources of funding."

Lucan's brow raised. "Oh?"

Olvin's gaze gleamed. "Let's just say that, like Drustan, she has many eager suitors. And she is in no hurry to make a choice."

Lucan's eyes again became cold and distant.

I looked along the partially-done shoes. A finely-made pair of men's leather boots, with beautiful ivy scrollwork, were about half-way finished. "Who are those for?"

Olvin's eyes sparkled with mischief. "Oh those? Those are for Pride."

I couldn't help it. I burst out laughing.

Lucan was watching me with an emotion I found it hard to name. And then he turned away, talking to Olvin. "Is Pride a newcomer to Lincoln?"

Olvin shook his head. "I only meant one of the three Deadly Sins."

I added, "It's what we all call the three apostles of Father Godwinson. I suppose he leads them all, representing Greed. But Pride certainly lives up to his name. When he's not wearing his robes, he can be found bedecked in all manner of exquisite workmanship."

Olvin's smile widened. "His sins are paving my way toward a better shop, that is for sure."

He glanced at Lucan. "Speaking of which, the man wants those boots by Sunday. Do you have any other questions for me? If not, I really have to get back to work."

Lucan moved toward the door. "Thank you for your time, Olvin. Let us know if you hear anything about the silver candlestick."

"Of course," Olvin said. "And, lad, it's good to have you back home again."

We waved and stepped outside.

Lucan stood for a moment, staring east, to where the city eased into farms and homesteads.

He murmured, "Anabel always did love green clover. Are you two still as thick as thieves?"

I moved to Rohesia without responding. I mounted up. In a moment he was on his own steed, alongside me.

I said, "Where to next, Reeve?"

He clearly noticed my evasion, but did not press it. He said, "The next person on Father Godwinson's list was Rudyard of Two Trees farm."

I snorted. "What a surprise."

I set out at a trot. Lucan kept right at my hip. He must have seen something in my eyes, for he did not ask a single question as we rode the fifteen minutes out to the farm.

The silence wrapped around me, as thick as autumn honey.

Chapter Four

We crested the hill over Rudyard's farm, and I could see Lucan's shoulders ease. Rudyard had been Lucan's family's next-door neighbor. The two families had helped each other during harvest's frenzy and kept each other company during the long winter nights.

Rudyard, fifty, portly, with tousled red hair, was out in his fields with his ox. He looked up with pleasure as he saw who was riding toward him. He strode over to the lane. "Lucan! Come and give me a hug. Look at you! You've grown!"

Lucan pulled up alongside him, easily dismounted, and the two men were in a bear hug. Then Rudyard turned to me. "Ah, it brings joy into an old man's heart to see the two of you together again. Two peas in a pod, you always were."

I blushed, and Rudyard brought me into an equally warm hug. He left the ox to graze and then walked with us back toward the main house.

"Francisca will be overjoyed to see you both. When did you get back, Lucan?"

"Just this morning. Lady Nicholaa asked me to help Father Godwinson -"

Fury boiled in Rudyard's face. "That blackguard! Do you know what he's done? Claimed my entire shipment of spring wheat was damaged in transport. Damaged! And he's only going to pay half of what he owes me! He threatened to send the Reeve out after me!"

Lucan gave that small smile of his.

Rudyard blinked in surprise. "Wait. Don't tell me. What about Reeve Bartholomew?"

"He had some sort of an accident. I wasn't told the details. I'd barely arrived in Lincoln when Lady Nicholaa asked for me to fill in until Bartholomew mended."

Rudyard spit into the weeds. "Which I hope is never. That man is a snake. I hear that he takes advantage of his station and pressures vulnerable women to – well - "

Pain coursed through me. I turned my head and stared out into the woods, my throat going tight. The men were suddenly both silent, but I did not turn. Our footsteps were the only sounds.

When Lucan spoke again, his voice was rough. "It seems that much has changed since I went away." He gave himself a shake. "How are your girls? I hear that Molly married my younger brother."

"And they have two fine boys, themselves," agreed Rudyard, warming back up again. "At this rate we might as well merge the two farms into one. We are back and forth on each other's properties enough."

He glanced over to Lucan. "I take it you haven't been to your own home yet?"

Lucan's eyes shuttered. "It's not my home any more. Zeke is taking fine enough care of it, with my parents."

Rudyard's voice grew tender. "Ah, lad, they miss you. They'll just be happy to have you back."

Lucan's voice was short. "I'm not back."

I turned in surprise.

It was hard enough riding by his side – but was he not staying?

He studiously did not look at me. "I'd been tasked to deliver an important message to Lady Nicholaa, since I knew the lands well and could navigate the way quickly. But I didn't intend to stay. This Reeve assignment is just temporary. Just until Bartholomew mends."

My voice caught in my throat.

He was leaving.

We had reached the farmhouse door, and we tied the two horses up to the rail. Rudyard welcomed us in.

I'd been here a number of times in my youth, and I'd always been impressed with how warm and welcoming the place was. Rudyard and his wife had raised five children, and now only the youngest still lived with them.

The house echoed with silence.

Rudyard saw me glancing toward the kitchen. "They're out in the city," he informed me. "Doing some shopping. They're probably stopping by your father's shop while they're there, to pick up some meat for the stew."

I nodded. Our family shop was often sought-after for their high-quality meats. It's how my family could afford to eat like kings.

And Drustan would inherit all of that. Because he was the boy-child.

Rudyard went to pour some wine, and brought us back three wooden mugs. "A toast. To the reuniting of old friends."

Out of habit, I did not look into the circle of liquid. Only at the side of the mug as I lifted it.

My eyes caught Lucan's.

He was already planning on moving on.

What was next on his schedule? Germany? Rome? Athens?

Lucan broke the gaze and looked away.

Rudyard clinked his mug into ours, then took a long drink. He put down his mug on the table. "All right, then, Reeve. Did Father Godwinson send you to harass me about that spring wheat?"

Lucan had been staring out the window at the meadow where he and I used to play tag. He turned with a blink. "No. We are here on different business. It's about a silver candlestick."

Rudyard snorted. He waved a hand around his room.

Everything in the room was carved out of wood. We were drinking from wooden mugs. Wooden plates sat on shelves above the plank table. There were wooden spoons hanging in a rack. There were a few wooden chairs along with plump hay-filled pillows.

Rudyard laughed. "What do you think, we're made of money? A silver candlestick on our table would stick out like … like a golden beak on a swallow!"

A hint of amusement lit Lucan's gaze, and he nodded.

I quietly said, "It's not just any silver candlestick, Rudyard. It's one of the etched lily candlesticks from the sacristy."

Rudyard's eyes went wide, now, and he rounded on Lucan. "Could you imagine in a million years that I would ever touch something like that? A holy object?"

Lucan put his hands up. "I am simply following Father Godwinson's instructions, Rudyard. Checking through a list of suspects."

Rudyard scoffed, "And who was on the top of that list? Olvin, I suppose?"

Lucan had the grace to tint his cheeks. He nodded.

Rudyard shook his head. "I hate to speak ill of a man of the cloth, but some men were never meant to be priests. You know why Father Godwinson took the vows, don't you? He was the second son. His older brother inherited the estate, and what is a second son to do? Go into the priesthood and rise as high as he can."

Lucan said, "My younger brother never felt that calling."

Rudyard's laugh was full. "Well that is different, isn't it? And, besides, you went off soldiering. He had the farm to tend to. And now he's got a family of his own."

Lucan's eyes went again to the meadow. I wondered what he was remembering.

The mornings we chased each other around, shrieking in delight.

The afternoons we lay in the grass, peacefully watching at the drifting clouds.

The evening he took my hand and vowed to never leave me …

Lucan asked Rudyard, "Who else had access to that candlestick?"

Rudyard shrugged. "Father Godwinson has those three acolytes working for him, the Sinners, but none of them are *greedy*." His mouth turned down. "That sin lies with Father Godwinson himself. The most miserly man in Lincoln."

Lucan frowned. "Does anyone else have easy access to the sacristy?"

Rudyard chuckled. "You'd have to ask someone who's allowed to get within fifty feet of it. Is anyone on that *list* of yours in that category?"

Lucan gave a small smile. "Would Quentin qualify?"

Rudyard's grin stretched ear to ear. "Absolutely."

Chapter Five

Quentin's forge was high on a hill overlooking Lincoln, on the opposite side of the city from mine. It was a full half hour's ride there from Rudyard's farm, and not one word was said during that ride. Lucan's gaze was shadowed, and I felt no need to break the silence.

Lucan had not hesitated one moment as we rode away from his family farm. He did not spare one glance in their direction. I wondered if he had so easily put away his past.

His family.

Me.

At last we drew near the forge, with the black smoke tumbling into the sky and the loud clanks of hammer on anvil ringing out across the fields.

We tied up the horses and walked in.

Quentin, burly, scarred, in his late forties, was just quenching a sword in a vat of oil. The steam rose hard off of it in a long hiss. Quentin then held the sword aloft, checking it carefully for any warp.

His eyes lit when he saw Lucan in the entryway. "Lucan! There you are! One of the soldiers told me you'd come to town, and that you had a fine Toledo sword on your hip. Let's see it!"

Lucan put a hand to his hip and in a smooth draw he had the sword laid out on top of Quentin's workbench.

Quentin's eyes went wide, and he walked along its length admiring it. "Now that is exquisite workmanship! Look at the etching near the pommel. And that engraving along its blade. *Fides et pietas*?"

Lucan said, under his breath, "Faith and loyalty."

I turned to stare into the fire. Had I imagined it, or was there an edge to his words?

Quentin's lips pressed, and he rounded on Lucan. Quentin was never a man to mince words or to step back from a confrontation. "Now, lad, you've been away a while, so I'll give you some rope. But what this young woman has endured, these past ten years, goes beyond any fancy phrases on that sword of yours. First her daughter, and then her husband."

Lucan blinked in shock. He rounded on me. "You had a daughter?"

My entire body felt constricted by iron bands. I could only nod.

Quentin said, more compassionately, "Only four years old, she was. The same age my youngest is now. If I lost little Emma like that, I don't know what I'd do. No wonder it drove Elric to take his own life."

Lucan paled. "God's teeth, Constance. I had no idea."

Quentin ground out, "Of course you didn't. You just rode in here on that fine horse and started casting judgments around. You used to be one of us, Lucan. You used to know better."

Lucan was still finding his breath. Slowly, he nodded. He murmured, "You're right, of course. My apologies, Constance. For all you have endured."

There had been a time in my life when I would have run into his arms. When I would have wrapped myself in the safety of his embrace and never let go.

But ten long years had passed …

Quentin turned fully to him. "All right, then. Let's get to the issue at hand. What did you really come out here for? Was it about that damned candle holder the Father is all wound up about?"

A slight tint came to Lucan's cheeks. He said, "I have been assigned acting reeve by Lady Nicholaa, while Bartholomew -"

Quentin spit on the ground. "Bartholomew deserved every bit of that injury, and much more besides. If I'd have come on him taking advantage of my wife -"

The fire in his eyes told the story.

Lucan's gaze hardened. "If Bartholomew is truly a rapist, then he should be brought to justice!"

Quentin barked a laugh. "None will go on record speaking out against him. And the man has powerful friends on high, protecting him."

Lucan's voice went still. "Lady Nicholaa?"

Quentin blinked. "No, no. If the Lady was ever presented with solid proof, I have no doubt she would flay the Reeve alive. But Bartholomew chooses his victims carefully. People who cannot risk speaking publicly."

My throat went tight. I looked down into the pool of water by the fire.

My vision dissolved ... unfocussed ...

I saw the small skeletal hand, deep in the earth. Its delicate fingers curled –

I sharply turned away, my eyes filling with tears.

My little butterfly –

Lucan said, his voice rough, "Connie, are you all right?"

I wiped at my face. "I'm fine." My eyes flitted around the forge, looking for something – anything –

I pointed at the leather belt with metal studs hanging on a rack. The workmanship was exquisite. "Is that for Gluttony?"

Quentin chuckled. "It is indeed. And that damned acolyte shepherd gets wider by the month. All the while his *flock* turns to skin and bones."

Lucan asked, "You must have a place near to the sacristy. Have you seen anyone else get near those candlesticks?"

Quentin shook his head. "Father Bartholomew protects few things in life as well as his silver set. Only him and his three acolytes ever get anywhere near those pieces. And he locks them up tight in a chest when they are not in use. He carries the key around his neck."

He spit again into the forge.

Lucan nodded. "All right, then. Maybe we should go have a talk with the three acolytes."

Quentin's laugh was sharp. "You think any of those miscreants would ever admit to the truth? They are as thick as thieves. I doubt you'd find any luck on that course."

"All right, then, do you think it would be Pride? Or Gluttony?"

Quentin immediately shook his head. "Pride is all about flashy fashion. He wants his personal appearance to show his mark as an elite man. Few people ever see his chambers in the castle. I doubt he wastes any money on that."

I chimed in. "And Gluttony is only buying that belt because, without it, his pants would fall down. His money all goes to the best wines and rarest ales. He wouldn't care one whit about candlesticks."

Lucan's brows came together. "All right, then. Who does that leave? Sloth? Wrath?"

Quentin's gaze was rich with amusement. "Why, I thought you knew."

Lucan's face was blank.

Quentin leant forward. "He's a good friend of your old pal, Anabel. He's the one we call *Lust*."

Chapter Six

Lucan and I walked alongside our horses, leading them along the eastern road back toward Lincoln. The sun was in that balanced position of edging between late day and early evening. The sky hinted at crimson and orange.

My bees would be meandering their way back to their hives –

Lucan said, in a low voice, "I'm sorry to hear about your husband and daughter. I can't imagine what that must have been like, to endure those losses."

His voice was so tender … so compassionate … to hear the words coming from his lips, after all these years, sent powerful waves of emotion through me.

I focused on my breath.

In.

Out.

At last I found words. "Elric took Juliana's death hard. We only were graced by her presence for four short years. Elric adored her. Maybe in the end it was the only possible outcome, that Elric would choose to join her."

When he spoke again, there was a new roughness. "It seems much has happened since I left Lincoln."

"And I imagine you endured a lot, in the Holy Land."

His gaze shadowed, and he looked away.
We both had our burdens to bear.

He gave a small smile as he looked down the road. "At least you weren't alone. I imagine you had Anabel by your side at every step. You two were always thick as thieves."

I pressed my lips together. "We were close, once."

He blinked in surprise. "You two were peas in a pod. What happened?"

"It was nothing."

He stopped walking and turned to me. "Connie, it's me. Lucan. I know how close you two were. It must have been *something*, to drive you apart."

His throat tensed, and his voice was lower when he continued. "Surely it wasn't simply about you marrying Elric. She was always eager for you to *marry rich*."

There were so many dense emotions wrapped up in that phrase. My parents' avarice. Anabel's hot jealousy. My own desperate helplessness.

And Lucan ... Lucan's eyes when I told him the news of my betrothal. Of the loss of all hope we had for a future together.

I shook my head. "Anabel turning from me didn't have to do with my marriage to Elric. It wasn't about anything I did. Rather ... it was about something I *didn't* do."

His gaze held mine with that insightful steadiness.

I had forgotten how well he knew me.

He said, "It involved your gift, didn't it."

He made it a statement rather than a question.

I sighed. At last I nodded. "Yes."

"Let me guess. She had a scheme involving money or position. And you refused to go along with it."

I blinked in surprise. "She told you?"

He gave that small smile. "No, I haven't seen her since arriving back in Lincoln. But I know what Anabel was like. And I know *you*."

Hearing those words sent warmth coursing through me.

He *had* known me. He had known me better than any other person alive. Better than my mother or father. Better than Anabel, even.

At last I nodded. "For years, Anabel stared into every pool of water, every full bucket, trying to see the things I saw. Trying to gain glimpses of the future. But when all her efforts resulted in failure, she decided that the next best thing was to make better use of my …"

The word *curse* sprang to mind.

His voice was soft. "Gift. You have a gift."

"Not all would see it that way."

His tone grew tight. "When you *saw* the chandler as your husband, I thought we could defeat it. I hoped we could make use of the knowledge and change fate." His jaw set. "But clearly your visions don't work that way."

I could see Juliana struggling to breathe … struggling to breathe …

He stepped closer and took my hand. "God's teeth, Connie, what is it?"

I shook my head and pushed the hair back from my eyes. "When I was young, my visions seemed intriguing. Useful, at times, even. But on the day my daughter was born, nine years ago, all other visions left me. I was left with one all-encompassing, all-consuming sight."

"About your daughter?"

My gaze dropped.

He nodded. "I can't imagine any other person you would have felt that strongly about."

There had once been a person I loved with all my heart ...

With effort, I pushed the thought away.

His voice became low. "What was the vision?"

It was so comfortable talking with him. He had always been my rock. My foundation.

And then he had been gone ...

His throat grew tight, and he looked away. "I'm sorry. I did not mean to presume -"

I laid a hand on his arm. "It's all right. It's just ... it's been a long time since I had someone to talk with about my visions. Someone who understood."

His shoulders eased, and he nodded.

I drew within myself. Slowly, carefully, I immersed myself in that inner world.

My shoulders hunched in of their own accord. "From the moment Juliana was born, all other Sight fled. This one was the only vision I saw. I saw it in the lily pond beyond the meadow. I saw it in the rusted bucket of water as it sat by the stable door. It was always the same."

Even all these years later, the image had the power to stop my breath. I forced myself to draw in air. "My daughter, in the cusp of her young childhood, choking. Unable to breathe."

Lucan blew out an oath. "God's teeth, Constance. I'm so sorry."

My gaze went to the road ahead. "You know as well as I do that my visions have always been unchangeable. Immutable. And yet, I tried. God knows how I tried. Everything I fed to Juliana, I cut into small pieces. I made sure any place she played was free of stones or small sticks. The closer we got to that apparent age, the more frantic I became."

A low laugh escaped me. "Elric called me *broken*. He dismissed my fears as a mother's foolishness, which only made my panic worse."

Lucan's voice was low. "What happened?"

We were in farmland. All around us was the lush, rich dirt, basking under the summer's sun. Long rows of grain waved in the wind.

After Juliana's death, I had spiraled into a dark, deep hole of agony and despair. My vision had changed with my descent. Gone were her auburn curls and bright green eyes. The new vision had shown only her skeletal hand, lost, alone, submerged in the dirt.

My beautiful butterfly ...

Elric had clung to that vision as a man obsessed. After having dismissed my previous Sight, he was wholly focused on following this one through. He refused to put our daughter into a coffin or even a shroud. He insisted she be buried at the base of the apple tree, well within sight of anywhere on our property. He remained nearby at all times.

He took to sleeping on the grave, regardless of rain or hail.

And then ... in the final stage of his grief ...

Lucan's voice was a rough whisper. "Connie?"

I gave myself a shake. "Come. It will be evening soon. Let us get on to Anabel's home and see if we can finish this up."

He looked as if he might press me for more, but at last he nodded. He helped me up onto Rohesia's back, and then with a press he was mounted alongside me.

We rode in silence as the tangerines eased into violets ... as the road moved beneath us ... and it was like old times, like when we were young ...

A woman cheerily called out, "Hallo!"

I looked up, wiping at my eyes.

A blonde in a clover-green dress, just about my age, was leaning against the sturdy fence which circled her elegant daub-and-wattle house. I knew there were a full three bedrooms within, even though it was just her and her mother living there.

All of Lincoln knew this tale. Anabelle's beauty was legendary. She had no shortage of wealthy men willing to support her lavish lifestyle, in hopes of claiming her as their own.

And she was always on the prowl …

Anabel's gaze sparkled with interest as she drew in the finery of Lucan's horse and gear. Her voice was sultry as she called over, "Well, welcome home, Lucan. You are a truly sight for sore eyes."

Chapter Seven

Lucan looked up at Anabel, blinking against the scene. I saw him take in the beautifully kept house, the elegant shutters, and the finely maintained rose garden.

I saw him look over the curvaceous blonde before us. I saw him take in the finery edging her tunic and the delicate precision of its tailoring.

I could see the surprise flash in his gaze, quickly masked, as he replied, "Anabel, I hardly recognized you."

It was true. When we were fourteen, Anabel had been a larvae slow to hatch. She had been smaller and frailer than the other girls in our group.

But fate had been bountiful to Anabel. She had taken after her delicately-formed mother, in that respect. Her mother, in her day, had been one of the most stunning women in all of Lincoln. She'd married a wealthy merchant and spent half of her time at Lincoln Castle, eating at Nicholaa de la Haye's table, hob-nobbing with the landed gentry. After Anabel's father had passed, her mother's reputation had grown by leaps and bounds. It had only been her poor health these past few years which had at last confined her to her bed.

But where Anabel's mother had been a vision of authentic beauty, Anabel herself was a deliberate construction. Every drape of fabric, every artful application of berry juice or clay powder, was specifically designed to draw in whoever had the largest purse. She was a stunning crimson rose in a field of pale columbine.

And with the way she was sizing up Lucan, she had a new target in her sights.

She purred, "I have some of the finest mead, just arrived from Canterbury. Your arrival home is surely cause for celebration, Lucan. Come, join me for a cup."

He glanced at me, his eyes echoing concern.

Anabel chimed in, "Oh, Connie is welcome, too, of course. It's been simply a lifetime since we last talked."

I turned to the blonde, forcing a smile onto my lips. "Yes, Anabel, thank you for your kind offer. We'd love to come in for a glass of mead."

Clearly Anabel wasn't going to miss out on her opportunity. Her smile could have lit the entire nave of Lincoln Cathedral. She swept her front gate open. "Right this way!"

We dismounted and brought our horses over to her stables. The building was large and well-kept. A young boy of perhaps eight ran out to help us as we removed the saddles and gear. By the efficiency of his movements, he had steady work handling horses of all shapes and sizes.

I stumbled as I turned, and Lucan caught my hand.

I looked up -

Our faces were inches apart.

His eyes were liquid pools which drew me into their depths.

The vision rose effortlessly before me, mirrored in those twin pools.

I knew the scene by heart. This vision had haunted me ever since my daughter had died. This vision had driven my husband Elric to brutal suicide.

Dirt. Lush, rich dirt. A slender, skeletal hand curled in that dirt. A skeletal hand which made Elric envision his beloved child alone, so alone, beneath the surface of the earth. The vision had driven him into madness. Into death.

By habit I began to turn away. I could not contain the grief of the loss of my beloved daughter.

Lucan said, softly, "Connie."

I breathed.

I felt his hand on mine.

In that breath, the scene took on almost a serenity.

My daughter was at rest. At peace. Surely she was now in God's welcoming embrace.

Lucan's hand was warm, secure.

My shoulders eased.

If this were to be my only way to see my daughter, I should find gratitude that I had this moment to treasure. Her small hand. Her delicate fingers –

My breath held.

I had never drawn in the vision like this before. I had never been this attentive to its details. But now that I looked, now that I paid closer attention, I could see something in the ring finger.

The bone was broken in two places.

My daughter had never suffered such an injury.

The truth of it swam over me in baffling awareness.

This was not my daughter.

Chapter Eight

Lucan's brow creased. He said in concern, "Connie?"

I gave myself a shake. I was not sure what I had just seen. It didn't make any sense. Maybe I was simply exhausted. Not seeing straight.

Anabel bounced over to us, knifing between us and taking a hand on each side. "Come on, you two. Let me show you what I've done to the house!"

She enthusiastically led us past the bountifully-planted herb garden and in through her carved front door.

My mouth fell open.

Elric had not been a miser by any stretch of the imagination. Our home featured two bedrooms and our bed was solid oak. The yew crib had been brought all the way from London. Our copper pots were finely detailed with tendrils of engraved ivy.

But Anabel's furnishings were many steps beyond.

A stunning tapestry depicting a man and woman on an arched bridge hung on one wall. Several intricately-carved marble figurines of deer and boar lined her mantlepiece. A sideboard held a matching set of six etched glasses, with cobalt-blue rims, along with a decanter.

The floor was polished wood.

A wolfskin rug lay before the stone fireplace.

She grinned, taking in my reaction. "A far cry from where we started, eh, Connie?"

She walked over to the sideboard and opened the doors beneath it. She drew out a corked bottle and placed it on top. She commented over her shoulder, "This bottle is probably worth more than that fine horse of yours, Lukki. I was planning on saving it for a special occasion. This would be it!"

He nodded without comment.

She poured the amber liquid into three of the beautifully etched glasses. Somehow with outstretched fingers she managed to put the three into a triangle and bring them over to us. Lucan took his first, then I took mine.

Anabel's eyes gleamed. "Look at us three. Who'd have thought it." Her gaze sharpened, and her lips pursed.

For a moment, she looked like the old Anabel. The one from my youth.

Her tone edged. "Well, you probably *did* see this all, didn't you, Constance. You just refused to share the information with me."

I shook my head. "I never saw any visions about you, Anabel. I would have told you. You know that."

Her mouth pressed flat. "Would you have?"

My eyes drew down to my mead.

The gold practically glowed from the glass. I wondered idly what nectar the bees had feasted on.

Anabel gave a rough laugh. "Then again, you've never made mead, have you, Connie? That husband of yours was so good with the bees, but he was afraid of the nectar of the gods." She took a long swig.

Lucan's eyes darkened. "Elric's father was a violent alcoholic, Annie. The whole city knew of his moods. It's a miracle Elric's mother made it to age thirty before she died."

Anabel shrugged, drinking again. "Mead brings in good money. But what did Elric do, the moment he took control of the hives? He sold every last piece of mead-making equipment. Lost a steady flow of cash, he did. Foolish."

Lucan's lips pressed flat, and I could see the tight line of his jaw.

Elric had never spoken to me of his mother nor father. Not once. Both had been long dead by the time I joined his household. Similarly, there had never been a drop of mead in our home the entire decade I had lived there. It was funny how an entire business operation centered around bees was lacking such a key component of its process.

I dropped my gaze. I'd forgotten just how glowing mead could be. The surface of the mead was rich … so rich …

I saw the deep, dark earth.

The skeletal hand.

The ring finger, broken in two places.

I had not been mistaken. The vision was clear.

It was not Juliana.

But who was it?

Something niggled at my mind about the injury. But what?

Anabel eased closer to Lucan. "You must have seen so many amazing places on your trips, Lucan. You were in the Holy Land. What an adventure that must have been! Did you visit Acre?"

Lucan's gaze had shuttered, and his jaw had gone tight. He nodded.

Anabel didn't see or didn't understand Lucan's mood shift. She blithely tripped onward. "Walter says Acre has all the best taverns. He's told me all about it. He was a crusader, you know, before he took the cloth. Now, of course, he's second only to Father Godwinson himself!"

Lucan glanced at me in awareness.

I nodded.

Lust.

Lucan said, "Anabel, do you know anything about -"

A memory snapped into place.

I interrupted, "Anabel, back when we were seven, do you remember your mother's riding injury?"

Anabel seemed flummoxed by the two intersecting conversations, but she turned to me. She drank down the rest of her mead and poured herself another glass. "Of course I remember. You and I were out racing our leaf-boats down the stream. When we got back home, Mother was in the kitchen, splinting her right hand. She said the horse had thrown her."

Her mouth turned down into a frown. "It made no sense to either of us. That horse was as sweet as a caterpillar. And besides, my mother was one of the finest horse riders in the city."

A cold chill went down my spine. "It ended up that she'd broken her ring finger, hadn't she? In two places?"

Anabel nodded. "She could never wear rings on that finger after that. It bothered her to no end."

She gave a small laugh. "Silly issue to worry about, though. After all, we've got nine other fingers to adorn."

Lucan's gaze attentively came to mine. He asked, "Connie, what is it?"

I lifted my gaze to look straight into Anabel's wide blue eyes.

I asked, steadily, "Anabel, where is your mother?"

There was a flash in her eyes. It was just for an instant, just for the wingbeat of a bee, but it had been there.

Then the warm smile returned. "I know she would love to see you again, too, Connie. Both of you. But I'm afraid she's not feeling well. She's quite ill. She doesn't want anyone to see her in the state she's currently in."

Lucan's gaze was honed in now. He drew to his feet. "I haven't seen your mother in ten long years, and I feel it only right to offer her my respects. She was always kind to me, when I was younger."

Anabel's gaze dripped compassion. "You were always so gentle-hearted, Lucan, to remember such things."

She sighed. "My mother's health has been declining for a while. I think all those years of high living finally caught up with her. She's now resting comfortably in her room. She naps, mostly, and wishes not to see any visitors."

My gaze went to the elegant tapestry … to the figurines on the mantle … to the long table before the sofa …

My eyes sharpened.

A grouping of five candles sat there. The four outer candles were pillars of the finest beeswax. Not mine – I had not seen Anabel since that summer ten years ago when we'd had our fight. Clearly she had gone elsewhere for her wax needs. But the centermost candle …

I cautiously stepped toward it.

Anabel's smile grew brighter. She downed her mead and refilled her glass to the very brim. "A toast! To old friends! To new beginnings!"

I pointed at the candle. "Lucan?"

He immediately came to my side. His brow creased. "That's a silver pedestal candlestick holder."

Anabel's laughter grew tinny. "Oh, yes, silver. I have any number of silver items in the house, of course. Silver knives, silver goblets, silver necklaces -"

He said, "This came from the sacristy. The engraving style on the pedestal matches that of the snuffer and trimmer."

Part of me was impressed that he was able to remember such level of detail. Another part of me was reminded of just how keen his mind was.

He turned slowly to face Anabel. "Anabel, where did you acquire this candlestick?"

Anabel's mead sloshed as she waved her hand around in quick motions. "That thing? I have so many pieces that it's hard to remember who gave me any particular one."

I lowered myself to one knee, staring with fixed attention at the tallow pillar.

Lucan said, "Connie?"

I gently poked at the edge of the candle. I inhaled deeply.

Anabel's mead had spattered on her beautiful green outfit. She seemed not to have noticed. "Maybe I can get you some cheese -"

I asked, "What type of fat is this from?"

A burst of laughter, high and sharp, shook her. "I don't know what you mean."

I touched it again, examining its color. "It's not calf. Not beef. No, and not pork, either. But with this texture, that can't be goat. Maybe mutton …"

She backed up toward the tapestry. "I'm not sure what you could …"

A chill ran down my spine.

I had a sense just what kind of fat had been melted to create this particular texture of tallow.

Just what kind of a *body* had been rendered.

Chapter Nine

I stared at the tallow candle before me, nestled in its finely engraved silver holder on the polished oak table. This was a candle like no other. A candle formed from a fat which I had never before seen formed into a taper.

Part of me, a morbidly fascinated part of me, wanted to reach out and touch it again. To see just how it compared with beef. With lamb. With pork.

For it was clearly none of those things.

My voice was hoarse as I said, "Lucan, please go check upstairs."

There must have been something in my tone; my face. For Lucan did not hesitate. He headed for the stairs.

Anabel flung herself at him, her glass mead goblet crashing to the floor, but in mere seconds he was free of her. He took the steps two at a time.

Footsteps sounded from above, moving from room to room. A pause. Then they were coming down to us again. Lucan said, his face growing hard, "Nobody. There is nobody upstairs. Not a sign that the spare rooms have been used for months."

Anabel's titter was high now. Sharp. Fragile, almost. "Oh, my Mother must be at the apothecary's. I completely forgot. You know how it is."

I took a long, deep breath. I seated myself on the embroidered couch. I held my mead glass before me with two hands.

Anabel took a step forward. "Constance, surely you, of all people -"

Lucan took her arm, holding her back. His gaze came to mine.

He nodded.

I let my breath out, feeling the flow of the warm air past my lips. I looked down into my mead glass. I focused on the honey liquid. On the circle of gold.

On what lay beneath …

On the rich, deep, dark earth. On the skeletal hand. On the ring finger. It was broken in two places.

How had I never seen that before?

I hadn't *wanted* to see it. I hadn't wanted to look at all. I had tried to shut out the Sight, to block the vision.

I had assumed it was my innocent daughter's hand.

The Butterfly Beneath the Earth

I had assumed wrong.

I raised my vision higher … higher … up over the dirt …

A flower.

A flower with long, oval leaves. A plant with violet-rose trumpet blossoms.

I whispered, afraid of the vision dissolving into mist, "Belladonna."

Lucan was out the door before the word left my lips. It took me a moment to shake myself free of the Sight, to regain awareness of the room around me. Anabel stood stock still in the center of her luxurious living room, shards of broken goblet scattered around her.

I let her be. I headed out the door, turning to see where Lucan had gone to.

There – he was walking with a purposeful stride toward the stables.

I hurried after him. As I approached, I realized that he was on the right path. There, in the corner of the herb garden, was a large belladonna plant.

I nodded to myself as I took it in. Its presence made sense – women obsessed with beauty would often use creams and unguents with belladonna to dilate their eyes and pale their skin.

The garden's earth here was dark and rich.

Anabel had somehow drawn herself together enough to chase after us. She was babbling. "Did you want some of the plant for yourself? I could see why you might. I'm happy to pluck off some of its -"

Lucan had already found a shovel by the stable door. He began digging at the base of the plant.

Anabel's voice rose higher now. "It was a tragic accident. Tragic! And I knew how beloved she was in the community. In the castle, even! I couldn't bring myself to break so many hearts. So I hid her away. Just for a while, of course. Just until I could break the news gently, that she had gone in her sleep. It was best this way. Best for everyone, because -"

His shovel hit something. He dropped to his knees and brushed with his hands.

The bones were haphazard. Tumbled. They had been cut into small pieces, perfect for tossing into a large pot for rendering …

I staggered to the ground alongside Lucan.

Anabel's face sharpened. It turned crimson. Her voice became hoarse with fury. "I curse you, Constance the Chandler. I curse you to Hell. If you had followed my plan, none of this would have happened. It's all your fault. Everything is your fault!"

I closed my eyes.

I wrapped my arms around my chest, allowing the world to fall away.

Darkness.

Chapter Ten

The stone bench was rough beneath me. My gaze could not be drawn from the belladonna plant. From the tumble of earth beneath it. From the white glisten of bones.

For some reason, Anabel had kept her mother's hand whole. She had left that piece of the body connected while the rest had been separated and rearranged.

Lucan's voice was above me. "Connie, are you sure? I'd really rather you came with us. I need to bring Anabel to the castle. I have to hand her over to Nicholaa de la Haye. But I'd rather not leave you here alone."

"You'll be back soon, with the soldiers. And I … I would like to sit with Anabel's mother a while."

His gaze held mine. "You'll be all right?"

I nodded to him. "I will wait for your return."

His eyes became distant, and it was a long moment before he nodded. Then he was mounted, trailing the wrist-tied Anabel behind him on her own horse. They rode together toward Lincoln, becoming lost in the evening blues.

Time passed. The sun eased its ways down, oranges glimmered in the sky, and still I sat, gazing at the tumbled earth before me.

Anabel's mother.

All this while, it had been Anabel's mother reaching out to me, telling me of the fate which overtook her. I wondered just what had finally sent Anabel over the edge. Had it been how well respected her mother continued to be in the castle, while Anabel herself was treated as a mere upstart? Had it been a fight over Anabel's refusal to marry, preferring to draw an income from every man within reach?

We might never know the truth.

I thought of the house alongside me, with all its elegant silver fixtures and embroidered tapestries.

Every inch of the place had been coated with soot from those tallow candles. Every surface had been touched by its gleam.

I had held the clue in my vision. But I had never seen it.

The sky drifted into violets and blues, and at last I heard the sound of returning hoofbeat. Four soldiers rode a wagon. Lucan was alongside Father Godwinson. The priest was in his full regalia. Anabel's mother had been a wealthy donor to his cause. He was going to return the favor.

I drew to my feet as they approached, and I joined Lucan as he came alongside me. We stood behind Father Godwinson as he said prayers over the body. The stars were twinkling before the soldiers got to their work. They had brought an embroidered linen sheet with them, undoubtedly an offering by the priest. In short order the dirt and bones had filled its center.

Lucan went into the house carrying a large oak box. When he returned, one hand held the candlestick. In the other, the box seemed to hold more weight. I had no doubt what type of candles were held within.

Father Godwinson's eyes lit up as if it were Christmas and Easter rolled together into one. He reverentially drew the candlestick in close to his breast. "Thank you, Lucan. Your promotion to reeve was clearly a gift from God."

Lucan's eyes were even. "I could not have found it without Constance's help."

Father Godwinson barely offered a glance in my direction. "Be that as it may, it was your quick thinking which brought an ungodly murderer to justice. We will see her hanged in three days. The quicker the better."

I wondered if his desire for haste was based on a quest to see Lincoln cleansed of the foul taint or whether he was attempting to forestall any attempt by Anabel to call on her substantial support structure for assistance. Any number of wealthy men could be dragged down, if Anabel were allowed to talk.

Those men would pay quite well to have Father Godwinson hurry along the process.

Father Godwinson brought his treasured candlestick over to his saddlebag, tucking it within. Then he mounted. He looked down on Lucan. "You will report to me first thing in the morning. We must process the necessary papers and legalities as quickly as we can. We must get this Anabel situation handled and behind us."

Lucan coolly nodded. "I will be there. Nine sharp."

Father Godwinson tossed his reins and was in motion.

Lucan went to talk with one of the soldiers. In another few minutes, the soldiers and their wagon were rolling slowly in motion, following the father back on course toward Lincoln.

It was just me and Lucan left, with the full moon glowing large over the scene.

Lucan came over to me. Compassion eased into his gaze. "Connie, I'm so sorry you got caught up in all of this. I know you and Anabel had grown apart, but still, this can't be easy. To think she was capable of killing her own mother …"

I said, "I should have known."

He shook his head. "None of us could have known. She had changed so much over these past few years. I hardly recognized her."

I looked again at the rough earth. "I mean, I should have known who it was in the earth. I saw a vision."

His brow creased. "You saw Anabel killing her mother?"

"No. I saw a vision of a small, skeletal hand in dirt. It began appearing after Juliana passed away. I just assumed it was Juliana. It never occurred to me that it was anyone else."

I ran a hand through my hair. "If only I'd thought to look more closely …"

"You can't blame yourself," he soothed. "You were in grief. You had suffered a mother's worst nightmare. It's no wonder you misinterpreted the sight. How could you possibly have known it was a warning about Anabel's mother?"

His words did little to ease the torment in my soul.

Because of that vision, Elric had refused to bury my daughter in the church's cemetery.

Elric had slept on the grave.

Elric had killed himself.

Lucan's hand wrapped around mine. He said, roughly, "It's not your fault, Connie."

We stood together, beneath the stars, as the moon rose up until it was lost in the twinkling clouds, a pale, distant echo.

At long last, he turned to me. "Come, Connie. Let's get you home."

Home

Suddenly, I knew with crystal clarity what I had to do.

I said, "I want to sell the house."

He blinked in surprise and stepped closer. "Are you sure?"

I nodded. "The hives, the house, the barn, all of it. It was always Elric's dream. And I'm not sure it was even that. I think he was just saddled with it by his abusive father and never escaped. But *I* can, now. I can be free of it."

His throat went tight. "But what of Juliana?"

I held his gaze. "I would like Juliana … and Elric … buried by the pond behind your family home. Where we used to sit under the willow."

He was quiet for a long moment, and I waited

—

At last he nodded. "Of course. It would be our honor."

He took my hand. "You will be free, Connie. Free to do whatever you wish in life."

I gave his hand a squeeze. "You know how I used to make those leather pouches for you and Anabel? For our family members?"

"Everyone loved them," he agreed. "Friends kept asking for you to make one for them."

"We certainly had enough leather around the shop, and it's something I grew good at. But when I left home, of course, all of that came to an end."

"And now…?"

I nodded. "With the proceeds of the sale of the house and lands, I could buy a small shop within the city proper. I could start making pouches. Bags. Purses. Scabbards."

His gaze shone. "You would be wonderful at it, Connie. And I'd be honored to be one of your first customers. I've always wanted a proper scabbard for my sword. To have one made by you …"

I held his gaze. "It might take me quite a while, to ensure your scabbard comes out just right. To create the perfect fit." My breath caught. "Will you stay until the task is wholly complete?"

A smile lifted his lips and shone in his soul.

"As you wish."

Thank you for reading *The Butterfly Beneath The Earth.*

If you enjoyed this novella, please leave feedback on whichever systems you enjoy using. Together we can help make a difference!
Be sure to sign up for my free newsletter! You'll get alerts of free books, discounts, and new releases. I run my own newsletter server – nobody else will ever see your email address. I promise!
http://www.lisashea.com/lisabase/subscribe.html

Please visit the following pages for news about free books, discounted releases, and new launches. Feel free to post questions there – I strive to answer within a day!

Facebook:
https://www.facebook.com/LisaSheaAuthor

Blog:
http://www.lisashea.com/lisabase/blog/

Share the news – we all want to enjoy interesting novels!

Dedication

    To my Sutton Writing Group and Boston Writing Group. Both groups support and encourage me in all of my projects.

    To my bass-playing partner of over 25 years, Bob See, who supports me in everything I do.

    Most of all, to my loyal fans who support me on Goodreads, Facebook, and other platforms. It's because of you that I keep writing!

About the Author

I'd love to hear any feedback or comments you have on the story. Feel free to contact me!

Free Books

These books below are free on all platforms!

The Butterfly Beneath the Earth

DELUGE
A FLOOD MYTH SHORT STORY
1
LISA SHEA

LISA SHEA
A TIME TO MOURN A TIME TO DANCE
1

DEATH WATCH
LISA SHEA

The Proposal
A Romantic Short Story
Book 1 - NYC
LISA SHEA

THE SIDEWALK
LISA SHEA

CHARTREUSE
LISA SHEA

ARIES
1
Zodiac Maidens of Melk Short Stories
LISA SHEA

CINDERELLA
A Retelling with Strength and Courage
Courageous Heroine Fairy Tales - Book One
LISA SHEA

Cordelia
1
A Cornish Pixie in Whitinsville
LISA SHEA

JOURNALING BASICS
LISA SHEA
Writing a Vision Statement and Setting Goals
step by step strategies for reaching your dreams
LISA SHEA
Five Minute MEDITATION
LISA SHEA
YOGA for Stress Relief and Forgiveness
Lisa Shea
Ten Minute YOGA
for Stress Relief, Focus, and Renewal
Lisa Shea
CHAIR YOGA
for Children through Seniors
LISA SHEA
YOGA
Lisa Shea
for Traveling by Plane Train Bus & Car
Enjoy your Trip Relaxed, Serene & Energized!
Lisa Shea
SLOW BREATHING
to Reduce Stress, Ease Pain, Release Anxiety and Fight Dementia
LISA SHEA

CHAKRAS
In Yoga, Meditation,
and Stress Relief
Lisa Shea

MEMORY
Brain Training
Book 1: Amusement Parks
LISA SHEA

Romantic
LOVE
Poems
poetry
collection of
adoration
and
praise
LisaShea
RomanceClass

Green Living
SAVING WATER
Water your Garden while
Conserving our Water Supply
Lisa Shea

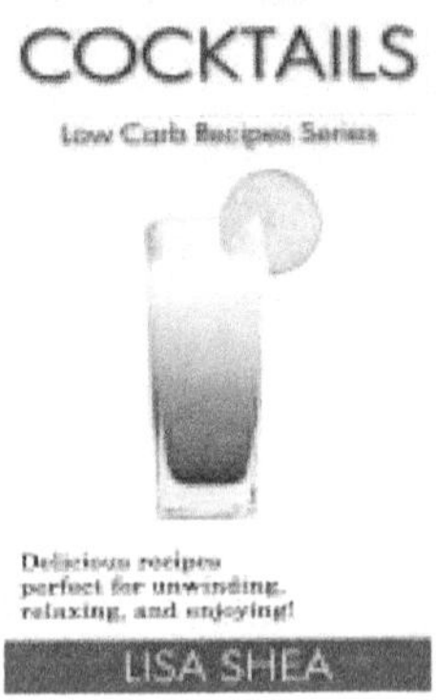
COCKTAILS
Low Carb Recipes Series
Delicious recipes
perfect for unwinding,
relaxing, and enjoying!
LISA SHEA

ART
SHOWS
How to Find,
Enter, and
WIN
an art show!
LISA SHEA

GETTING
REVIEWS
2021
LISA SHEA

I may have added more free books since releasing this list here. For the most up to date version, be sure to visit:

http://www.lisashea.com/freebooks/

Thank you for supporting the cause!
Be the change you wish to see in the world.

Printed in Dunstable, United Kingdom